This igloo book belongs to:

....

igloobooks

Published in 2013
by Igloo Books Ltd
Cottage Farm
Sywell
NN6 0BJ
www.igloobooks.com

SHE001 0713
2 4 6 8 10 9 7 5 3 1
ISBN: 978-1-78197-588-6

Printed and manufactured in China

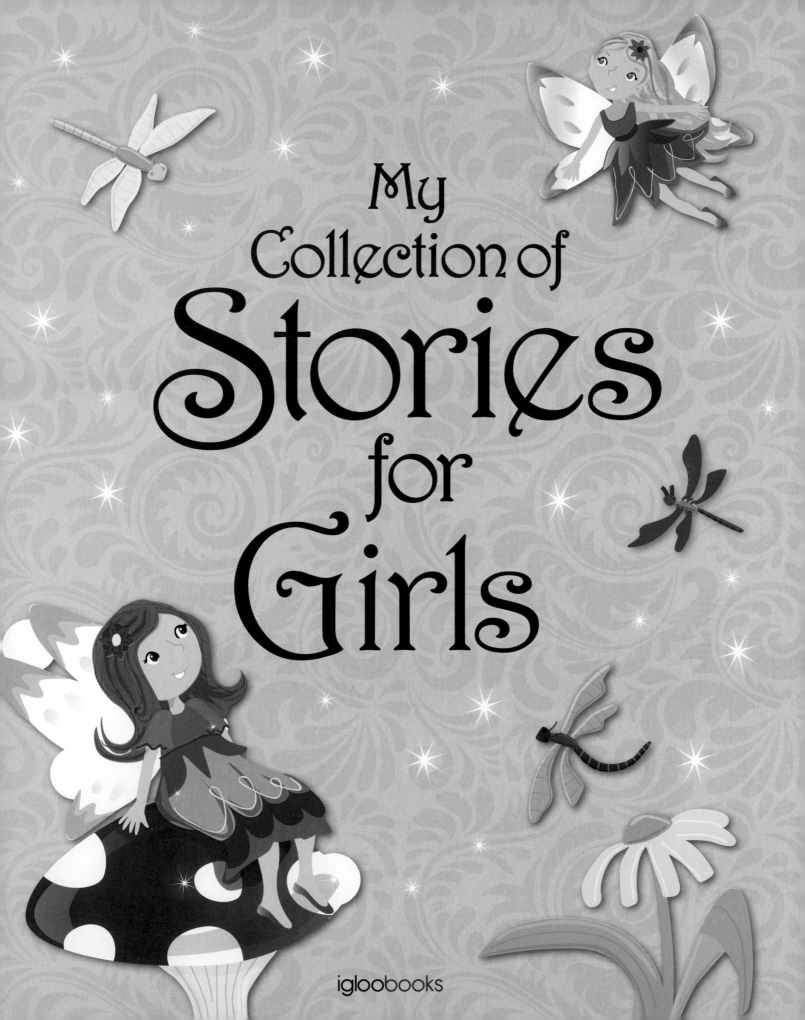

My Collection of Stories for Girls

igloobooks

Contents

Princess Crystal's Cleaner-Upper

Princess Crystal was fed up with the royal family. They were just so messy and lazy. The queen left her clothes lying around everywhere. The king never wiped his feet on the mat when he came in and her brother and sister never tidied away their toys.

It was the day of the royal ball and Princess Crystal was worried. "What will all the guests say if the palace is a complete mess?" she thought to herself. She opened her bedroom door and stepped out into the hall. Crystal gasped. "Oh, no!" she said. "It's even messier than usual."

As Crystal looked down the stairs, she could see paint splodges, muddy footprints all over the carpets and cobwebs hung from the ceiling. "How am I going to clean all this by tonight?"she thought.
"Don't worry," said the king, who was walking up the stairs. "We will do it later." Princess Crystal sighed. She knew her family wouldn't do it later. They were too lazy for that.

Luckily, Crystal was very good at inventing things. "I wonder if maybe I need to invent something to clean all this mess?" thought Princess Crystal. "It must be quicker than tidying it all up by myself."

Princess Crystal reached for her tool belt and dashed off to her royal workshop. Quickly, she set to work designing a machine to tidy up the palace in time for the grand ball.

The problem was, Princess Crystal's inventions didn't always work quite how they were supposed to. Once, she had built a Sunshine Maker that had made it rain for three weeks and another time, she created an Automatic Weeder that had pulled up the queen's best roses. However, she was sure that her latest idea would work perfectly. "I'll call it the Cleaner-Upper," decided the princess, as she tightened the last screw on her new device.

Princess Crystal couldn't wait to try out her new invention. She wheeled it straight to the kitchen and flicked the switch to turn it on. With a click and a whirr, the Cleaner-Upper sprang into action, wiping up crumbs, washing the dishes and sweeping away all the cobwebs.

Before long, the whole room was spotless. The silver cutlery sparkled and the white plates shone. Even the cereal boxes were lined up in a neat row. The princess was delighted. "The Cleaner-Upper will clear away all the clutter in no time," she said. "Everything will be nice and neat before the guests arrive tonight."

Crystal took the Cleaner-Upper all around the palace. It dusted and vacuumed, sorted and swept until everywhere was fresh and clean.

Soon, there was only one room left to tackle. The princess pushed the machine into the grand ballroom and switched it on. "This is my best invention ever," she said, as the clever contraption mopped the dance floor and polished the chandeliers at the same time.

Suddenly, the Cleaner-Upper started to tremble. It made a low rumbling noise that got louder and louder, until the princess had to cover her ears. Then, there was a loud bang and a cloud of dust, dirt, crumbs and cobwebs spurted out all over the ballroom.

Princess Crystal's Cleaner-Upper

"Now the ballroom is more untidy than ever," howled Princess Crystal, looking around her at all the muddle and mess. "I'll never get it cleaned up before the ball."

The rest of the royal family had heard the bang and rushed in to see what all the noise was about. When they saw how upset Princess Crystal was, they promised to help clear away the mess. "Sorry we have all been so lazy," they said. "We will be tidier from now on."

The queen pulled on her royal rubber gloves and started sweeping while the king polished until he could see his face in the shiny reflection. "What a handsome old fellow," he remarked, smiling at himself.

The royal family worked together all day long, tidying and cleaning the ballroom. They were just putting away their brooms and dusters when the guests started to arrive for the grand ball.

The queen quickly straightened her crown and brushed a couple of crumbs off the king's robe. The prince shook a cobweb out of his hair and the two princesses dusted down their dresses.

Then, the royal family gave their best sparkling smiles and, one by one, they welcomed their guests to the gleaming ballroom.

Soon, everyone was dancing and chatting and having a wonderful time. The band played tunes on their twinkling instruments while the guests nibbled tasty treats from the bright, clean plates. "I can't believe how beautiful it looks," said Princess Crystal as she admired the glittering chandeliers and shining dance floor.

The Cleaner-Upper may have been a disaster, but she had discovered something even better. "All you need to get things done is a bit of hard work," she said, "and a lot of teamwork!" Then, she put her arms around her family and gave them all a great big hug.

Lucy's New Doll

Lucy held up the small, yellow hoop and aimed it carefully at the shiny, glass jar. She was determined to win the sparkly doll on the hoopla stall. All she had to do was throw one of her three rings over a prize jar.

With a flick of her hand, Lucy sent the first ring flying, but it bounced off the side of the stall and fell to the ground. The next ring soared over the top and landed on the other side of the table.

Lucy picked up the last ring. "I wish I could win that doll," she murmured quietly. The doll seemed to glow softly as the ring spun round in the air and then dropped down over one of the jars. "I've won!" cried Lucy. The man behind the stall handed her the doll and she hugged it tightly.

The next day was bright and sunny, so Lucy took her new doll outside to play in the garden. She dressed the doll up and brushed her hair, then walked round the garden showing her all the pretty flowers.

After a while, Lucy sat down and sighed. "I wish I had a bouncy ball to play with," she said. "I'd love to play a game of catch."

The doll started to sparkle and at that moment, a pink and red ball flew over the garden fence and bounced across the lawn. "I wonder where that came from," said Lucy, picking it up.

Lucy threw the ball up into the air and caught it, then she bounced it on the ground. It was a very good ball, but it wasn't much fun playing with it all by herself. "I wish I had a friend to play with," she said, sadly. Lucy dropped the ball and picked up the new doll. It sparkled brightly in the sunshine.

Suddenly, a girl popped up on the other side of the garden fence. "Hello," she said. "Have you seen my ball?" Lucy smiled shyly and passed the pink and red ball over the fence. "My name's Anna," said the girl. "Do you want to play?"

The two girls had so much fun playing catch together, they didn't notice it was time for lunch until Lucy's belly started to rumble. She was just about to wish for a yummy picnic to share, when Anna's mom came out into the garden and invited her over for lunch.

Lucy's mom gave her some cakes to take with her to Anna's and the two girls were soon spreading out all the delicious food on a picnic rug. They even set out a plate of tasty treats for Lucy's new doll.

That evening, Lucy snuggled up in bed, cuddling her new doll. She thought about all the wonderful things that had happened since she had won her on the hoopla stall at the fair. "All my wishes have come true," thought Lucy. She gazed out at the twinkling stars in the dark night sky and decided to make one more wish. "I wish that we will always be together," she whispered to the sparkly doll.

The doll glowed softly in the moonlight as it granted the special wish, but Lucy didn't notice. She had closed her eyes and was smiling happily as she drifted off to sleep.

The Spooky Shipwreck

It was a lovely sunny day out at sea, but Coral, Marina and Shelly were feeling bored. The three friends perched on a rock, combing their long hair and flicking their shiny tails. "I'm tired of sitting on this rock and swimming round the same old reefs," said Coral. "It's time we found somewhere more exciting to play."

The mermaids thought for a long time. "How about a game of hide-and-seek in the seaweed forest?" suggested Marina. Coral shook her head.
"It's too dull there and the seaweed is all slimy," she said.
"Let's go and look for pretty shells near the sandbanks," said Shelly. "We could make them into necklaces."
"We did that last week," sighed Coral.

Suddenly, she had an idea. "Why don't we swim down to that spooky, old shipwreck?" asked Coral. Marina and Shelly looked at one another.
"I've heard that it's really dark and creepy down there," said Marina.
"It's supposed to be haunted," added Shelly with a shiver.
"At least it will be exciting!" said Coral. "Come on, I'll race you there."
Coral dived into the water with a splash and her two friends followed.

Down, down, swam the three mermaids, past the bright reef and the swishing seagrass, past the darting fish and the wriggling squid, to the very bottom of the sea. When they reached the old shipwreck, Coral was very excited. "Come on, let's go and see what's inside," she said. All around the sunken ship strands of slippery seaweed waved like long, curling tentacles.
"It looks scary," said Shelly, as she swam along behind the others.

Suddenly, Shelly noticed a strange, glowing light. "What's that?" she asked.
"I don't know," said Coral, "but I'm going to find out."

The Spooky Shipwreck

Coral swam through the ship's old, wooden door. It opened with a loud creak. Inside was a long corridor that echoed with strange sounds. Marina and Shelly shuddered as they followed their friend along the dark, winding passageway. "I think the noise is coming from in here," said Coral, tugging open one of the cabin doors. Swoosh! A shoal of little fish shot out, making them all jump. Shelley shrieked and tripped over an old barrel.

"It was just some clownfish," said Marina, helping her friend up.

"Well, that explains the noise," said Coral. "What about the strange light we saw?"

The mermaids followed the eerie glow until they reached the ship's grand ballroom. "It isn't very grand anymore," said Shelly. She looked round at the slimy walls and tattered curtains. The crystal chandeliers were hidden under a layer of green sea moss, but a bright shaft of light shone from an old chest in the middle of the dance floor.

"Let's see what's inside," said Coral, as she carefully lifted the lid.

The three friends gasped in amazement. The chest was full to the brim with sparkling jewels that glimmered and glowed with a bright light.

"We've found a treasure chest!" cried Coral, scooping up a handful of shimmering gems. Marina tried on a twinkling tiara, while Shelly covered her fingers in glittering rings.

"We can't keep it to ourselves," said Marina. "We've got to let everyone know."

Coral smiled and swished her tail excitedly.

"I've had a brilliant idea, but it's going to involve a lot of cleaning!"

So, the mermaids set to work scrubbing and polishing, sweeping and sewing. At last, the ballroom began to look grand once again. "Now we need to write some invitations. Let's ask everyone to come to a fabulous party!" said Coral.

The three friends sent off their invitations with some passing seahorses.
They swished off into the blue waves and, before long, all the mermaids and sea
creatures started to arrive.

Everyone was astonished when they saw how wonderful the old shipwreck
was looking, especially the magnificent ballroom. The walls were bright and clean
and the dance floor shone. Even the old curtains had been mended and the stage
was decorated with pretty shells. Coral handed each guest a piece of sparkling
treasure to wear at the party.

The ballroom was soon buzzing as the mermaids chattered and laughed together, their jewels glittering in the light from the shining chandeliers. "I can't believe we used to think that it was spooky here," said Shelly.

"I know," said Marina, happily. "It's the perfect place for a party." Coral floated up to her friends and gave them a big hug.

"Everyone is having a wonderful time," she said. "Now we have somewhere new to play, we will never be bored again!"

Twinkle's Special Talent

It was the day of the big talent show in the Fairy Kingdom and Twinkle the fairy was feeling sad. "There is nothing interesting that I'm good at," she thought to herself. "I wish I had a special talent."

Twinkle's friends were very clever. Her friend Fenella was a good singer, her other friend Lula was a good dancer and even Twinkle's sister, Eve, could play the flute very beautifully. The only thing Twinkle could do was fly and although she loved to fly, the thought of performing in front of everyone, especially the fairy queen, scared her. "Maybe I won't take part in the contest," Twinkle said, sadly. "I'll just go and play with the dragonflies instead."

Twinkle whizzed away and was soon doing daring double twists and loop-the-loops, while the dragonflies zipped along beside her. "Woo-hoo!" cried Twinkle, as the air whooshed past her face and blew out her hair in a long stream.

Twinkle was having so much fun, she didn't notice that Fenella was sitting on a toadstool nearby. Fenella looked up, saw Twinkle's spectacular stunts, stopped singing her song and stared, amazed at what she saw.

"I didn't know you could fly like that, Twinkle!" cried Fenella, as she watched her friend somersault over a sunflower. Twinkle was so surprised to hear Fenella's voice that her wings froze in mid-air and she tumbled to the ground. Squelch! She landed in the middle of a muddy puddle.

"Oh, please don't tell anyone," begged Twinkle, pulling herself out of the squidgy mud. She sat down next to her friend. "I just wanted to take my mind off the talent show." Twinkle explained how she had tried to think of something to do for the contest. "It's no good though," she sighed. "I just don't have a special talent."

30

Twinkle's Special Talent

"What?" gasped Fenella. "You have an amazing talent. You can fly wonderfully."
Twinkle looked doubtful. "I'd be too scared to do any of my tricks in front of everyone," she said. "What if I fall down again?"
"We all make mistakes," said Fenella. "You just need to keep trying."

Twinkle thought about all the tricks she had learned with the dragonflies.
"I suppose it might be fun to show one or two special moves," she admitted.
"It's time to stop hiding your talent," said Fenella firmly. "You should be proud of what you can do."
"You're right. I will fly at the talent show," decided Twinkle, feeling confident at last.

Twinkle fluttered off to a quiet woodland clearing. Taking a big, deep breath, she shot straight up into the sky then flipped over and dived down, down, down. She dived towards the ground but instead of concentrating on her flying, Twinkle started worrying about the show. "What if I mess it up and everyone starts to laugh?" she fretted.

Before she realised it, the little fairy was just inches above the tops of the flowers. "Oh, no!" cried Twinkle, as she tried frantically to slow down, but it was too late. She crashed through the flowers straight into a sticky web, sending a surprised spider scuttling away.

"Well, that wasn't a good start," grumbled Twinkle, pulling the sticky strands of web off her dress. "I'm not going to give up that easily though," she thought to herself.

Soaring back up towards the bright, blue sky, she decided to try out another one of her moves. Twinkle spun round in circles, performing perfect loop-the-loops. She shut her eyes tightly and imagined flying in front of the fairy queen. She could picture her sitting in the judge's chair, just waiting for Twinkle to make a mistake. Twinkle's eyes popped open, just in time to see a branch rushing up towards her. She bounced off it and was flung, face first, into a flower.

Twinkle was dusting the pollen from her dress when the fairy bells rang out to announce the start of the contest. There was no more time to rehearse. "I'll just have to do my best," she thought, as she waited nervously for her turn to perform. At last, Twinkle's name was called and the little fairy walked shakily out onto the stage.

Swooping up into the air to do her first loop-the-loop, Twinkle could feel the panic rising up inside her. "I'm bound to crash," she mumbled. Her wings began to wobble and she tipped to one side. Twinkle was about to fall when all of a sudden, she was surrounded by shimmering dragonflies.

The dragonflies darted around Twinkle, just like they did when she flew in the meadow. She closed her eyes and imagined herself whizzing through the flowers. "This is easy," she thought, beginning to relax. "I just have to concentrate on flying and forget about the audience."

Before long, Twinkle and the dragonflies were dazzling everyone with their daring flying display. Together they spiraled and soared through the sky. When they had finished, the crowd cheered and the fairy queen awarded Twinkle first place. "You are a very talented fairy," she declared, handing Twinkle a large, shiny, gold medal. Twinkle blushed.
"I couldn't have done it without my friends," she said, smiling at Fenella and the sparkling dragonflies. "They helped me to find my special talent."

The Fabulous Fashion Show

It was the day before the fashion show and Rosie arrived at school early to make sure everything was ready. Her class had spent weeks picking out the right clothes and trying out fancy hairstyles on each other. Now they were looking forward to strutting up and down on the stage and showing off their cool outfits, just like real models.

Rosie wanted to start organizing the clothes straight away, but when she popped backstage to pick up the boxes, she got a nasty shock. All the clothes had gone! "Where can they be?" she gasped. Rosie searched frantically through the piles of old props and theatre costumes, but there was no sign of the outfits. Spotting Mr Parker, the school janitor, she dashed over to ask him if he had seen the boxes of clothes.

"I'm very sorry, but the lorry has just taken all the boxes away," he said, shaking his head from side to side. "They were left by the back doors and that's where we put all the trash."
"This is a disaster!" cried Rosie. "What are we going to wear for the fashion show tomorrow?"

When Rosie's teacher, Mrs March, announced the bad news to the class, they all groaned with disappointment. "There's no time to find new outfits now," wailed Rosie's friend, Jess.
"Will we have to cancel the fashion show?" asked Rosie.

Mrs March was busy pulling things out of drawers and boxes. She turned and smiled at the class. "No, the show must go on!" she said, holding some scraps of material, ribbons and beads from the craft box. "We can have a recycled-fashion show," she explained. "Please bring in anything you can find at home that we can use to make some new clothes."

The next day, the class set to work designing a whole range of new outfits for the show. They cut up old T-shirts and sewed on sequins and beads. Trousers were turned into shorts and sweaters became vest tops. Even the sleeves were transformed into stylish leg warmers.

Everyone was having a great time and the room buzzed with chatter as the class shared ideas and discussed their new designs. Mrs March stopped by Rosie's table to admire the fabric she was decorating. "I think we are going to have some amazing outfits for the show tonight," said Mrs March.

That evening, as the show was about to start, Rosie peered round the stage curtain and watched the audience arrive. Parents and friends talked and laughed as they filled the hall, then as soon as the music started, everyone went quiet. Bright spotlights lit up the stage as the first models stepped out in their recycled outfits. The audience pointed and smiled as they saw how the class had given a new look to the old clothes and scraps of material they had sent in. "I hope Mom likes what I've done with her old fabric," Rosie whispered to Jess, as they waited for their turn to model.

At last it was time for Rosie to step out into the spotlight. She smiled and waved as she paraded down the stage, stopping to pose at the end before strutting back up.

After the show, all the parents came through to backstage. "That was amazing," smiled Rosie's mom. "How did you make that old fabric look so good?" Rosie and her friends explained how they had created the clothes for the fashion show. "I'm glad we made all the outfits ourselves," said Rosie. "Now we're just like real fashion designers."

Poppy's Puppy

Poppy felt really excited when she saw Dad's car pulling up outside the house. She ran to the stairs and shouted up to Mom, "Dad's back! Come on, Mom." "I'll be there in a minute," replied Mom. "I'm just looking for something." Poppy raced along the hall, nearly skidding on the rug as she went and dashed out of the back door. "Have you got him?" she called to Dad.

The car door clunked shut and Dad turned round. In his arms was the cutest puppy that Poppy had ever seen. He was golden brown with a white patch over one eye. "Meet the newest member of our family," said Dad. "His name is Scamp." "He's gorgeous!" cried Poppy. She stroked Scamp's soft little head and he wagged his tail.
"He likes you," said Dad. "Why don't you take him upstairs to show Mom?" Poppy held Scamp gently and took him upstairs.

"Look Mom, the puppy's here," said Poppy, going into her parents' bedroom. Poppy's Mom was busy emptying drawers. She looked at Scamp and said, "You'll have to make sure he behaves, Poppy. I'm busy looking for my wedding ring. I can't find it anywhere." Mom didn't seem interested in Scamp and Poppy was a bit disappointed.

Poppy decided to take Scamp into the garden to play, but he had other ideas. He wanted to explore his new home.

Scamp wriggled out of Poppy's arms and dashed down the stairs, his soft ears flapping as he ran. "Stop, Scamp!" cried Poppy, chasing after him. The puppy skidded round the corner into the hallway, knocking over the coat stand as he raced past. Coats, hats and scarves flew through the air as Poppy reached out to grab Scamp's collar, but he was just out of her reach and ran straight through into the living room.

Scamp jumped onto the sofa and bounced up and down on the seats, scattering cushions everywhere. Then he raced round the room, wagging his little tail with excitement. Bang! Scamp bumped into the coffee table as he hurtled past. Crash! A lamp toppled over and fell to the floor.

"Watch out!" Poppy shouted, but it was too late. Scamp dived for Dad's feet, yapping at him and tugging at his slippers. Dad started laughing, stepped back and ended up tumbling onto the sofa. "Aaaargh!" cried Dad as he fell onto the heap of cushions. "Oh, no!" gasped Poppy, "Come here Scamp, that's very, very naughty." Woof! barked Scamp and he dashed off to explore the kitchen.

45

There were so many exciting things to explore in the kitchen that Scamp didn't know where to start. He scrambled across the clean floor, knocking over the trash can and leaving a trail of garbage behind him.

Poppy reached the kitchen just in time to see Scamp tip over the bucket Mom had been using to clean the floor. Scamp bounded straight over it. He skidded across the floor and landed with a crash in a pile of shopping. Bananas, biscuits and toilet rolls burst out of the broken bags and covered the floor, mixing in with the contents of the trash can.

Poppy's Puppy

While Scamp was busy sniffing at the shopping, Poppy tiptoed across the room and grabbed hold of his collar. "At last," she sighed, pulling him firmly away from the broken biscuits. "Come here, you naughty puppy."

Just then, Mom came into the kitchen to see what all the noise was about. She was followed by Dad, who was looking a little cross. Poppy held on tight to Scamp as Mom and Dad stared around them at the chaos in the kitchen. They looked very angry and Poppy braced herself while she waited for them to start shouting.

Then, something strange happened. Instead of shouting, Mom started to smile. She was staring at the heap of trash that had spilled out of the trash can when Scamp knocked it over.

Poppy looked down at the mess and saw something glinting in the middle of the old teabags and potato peelings. Suddenly, she realised why Mom was looking so happy. "It's your wedding ring!" cried Poppy.
"It must have fallen off when I put something in the trash can," smiled Mom. She picked up the ring, cleaned it under the tap and slid it back onto her finger.
"Thank goodness I found it," said Mom.
"You mean Scamp found it," said Poppy confidently, with a cheeky grin.

Mom was so pleased to get her wedding ring back that she couldn't stay cross with Scamp. "If it wasn't for that naughty puppy I would never have found my ring," she said, picking up Scamp. She gave him a big hug and Scamp wagged his tail and licked her face.

Dad looked confused. "I'm not sure what's going on," he said, "but it seems like it's all turned out for the best." Poppy grinned and cuddled her Mom. "I think Scamp is going to be the perfect pet for us," she said and Scamp agreed with a happy woof!

The Scooter Race

Megan was enjoying spinning round and round on the roundabout at the park, until her big brother Harry jumped on to it. He landed with a thud and stood, grinning at Megan. "I can make this go much quicker than you can," he said, as he pushed the roundabout faster and faster, until Megan felt dizzy. Then, Harry smiled and pointed at the swings. "Come on, watch me swing the highest," he said, running off toward the swings.

Megan followed Harry and soon they were swinging backwards and forwards, getting higher and higher with each swing. "You can't beat me," cried Harry, teasing his sister.

Megan was fed up. Harry was always better at things than her. "I think I could beat you in a scooter race to the ice cream truck," she said, challenging him. "You're on!" said Harry.

They jumped on their scooters and lined up by the swings, ready to race. Megan knew Harry was fast on his scooter, but she was going to try her best. "Ready, steady, GO!" shouted Megan.

Megan pushed off with her foot and started rolling forwards, but Harry was faster. He raced away and was soon disappearing into the distance. "See you at the finish line," called Harry, over his shoulder, "if you make it that far!"

With a sudden burst of speed, he zoomed up a little slope and flew right over the top of the flower beds. "There's no way I can catch up with him," thought Megan, but she was determined not to give up. "Even if I can't win, I can still try my best."

Before long, Harry was so far ahead that he couldn't even see Megan. As he came up to the tennis courts, he saw a group of his friends playing basketball on the court next door. "Megan's so far behind me, I could just have one quick game," thought Harry. He put his foot against the back wheel, slowing his scooter down and skidded round and through the entrance to the tennis courts. Harry whizzed through the middle of the tennis match, much to the surprise of the players who had to jump out of his way. Swerving to dodge a tennis ball, he glanced back behind him, but there was still no sign of Megan.

"Come and play," called Harry's friend Zac, throwing him the basketball. Feeling sure he would win the race, Harry dropped his scooter and bounced the ball over to the court.

"I've got lots of time before Megan catches me up," he said with a grin.

Harry quickly joined the game. He was about to take a shot at the basketball hoop when Zac nudged him. "Hey, isn't that your sister?" he said, pointing at Megan. Harry's shot bounced off the edge of the hoop. He gasped in shock as he watched Megan gliding along on her scooter. She smiled and waved as she passed by.

54

Dashing out of the basketball court, Harry jumped onto his scooter and hurtled towards the ice cream truck. He scooted along at top speed, but it was too late. Megan was already there.

"I win!" cried Megan, as her brother skidded to a halt beside her.
"Well done," said Harry. "You did brilliantly and I know the perfect prize for a scooter champion." He went to the truck and bought her an ice cream with extra sauce. "I guess I'm not the best at everything after all," smiled Harry.
"Oh, I don't know," said Megan, thoughtfully licking her ice cream, "you're pretty great at being a big brother!"

The Spotty Pony

"Please can we go and see Sandy?" begged Alice, plonking down her suitcase. She had just got back from vacation with Mom and Dad and couldn't wait to visit the most beautiful, spotty pony she knew, Sandy.

Sandy lived at Evergreen Farm and Alice spent all her spare time there. It was fun feeding the goats and collecting eggs from the hen house, but what she loved best of all was riding Sandy.

The little pony's coat was light brown, with milky white splodges and she had soft brown eyes. Sandy whinnied with joy whenever she saw Alice and they spent hours trotting around the farm together. So, when Mom booked a vacation cottage for the whole summer, Alice knew she would miss Sandy terribly. Riding a donkey on the beach was fun, but it wasn't the same as riding Sandy. Now they were back though, Alice was beginning to worry that Sandy might have forgotten her. "We haven't been away that long," said Mom with a smile. "I'm sure she will remember you."

Alice grabbed an apple from the fruit bowl and they set off for the farm. She was so excited, she raced all the way to the paddock, but when she got there, it was empty. Sandy was gone.

Alice looked all around the field and checked in the stables, but Sandy was nowhere to be seen. "Where can she be?" wondered Alice as she set off to search for the missing pony.

Hurrying through the farmyard, she heard a clip-clopping sound coming from behind the barn. "It's Sandy!" she cried and skipped round the corner to see the pony, but it wasn't Sandy's hooves that she had heard. Buttercup the cow was passing by with a cute little calf trotting behind her. Buttercup called to the calf with a soft moo and together they clip-clopped off into the barn.

"How cute," said Alice, but she didn't stop to stroke the calf. She had to find Sandy. Before she could decide where to look next, Alice heard a snuffling sort of noise. It sounded just like a little pony munching on some hay. "That must be her," said Alice and followed the noise all the way to the pig pen.

Inside, all she found was a litter of piglets sniffling and snorting in the straw. Alice flopped down on a stool and watched the piglets snuffle around, their curly tails waving in the air. She was starting to wonder if she'd ever see Sandy again, when suddenly she had a brilliant idea.

"Farmer Fred must have moved Sandy to the meadow," said Alice. "She loves grazing there." So, Alice jumped off her stool and ran over to the meadow. It was full of green grass that looked juicy and sweet. It would make the perfect treat for a hungry pony.

Climbing up on the wooden gate, Alice peered across the meadow. She could see some fluffy, white sheep and lots of leaping lambs about the field, but there was no sign of Sandy. The lambs were so sweet and funny that Alice couldn't resist playing with them. They made her laugh as they hopped and skipped, but she still missed Sandy. Perhaps the little pony really had gone away.

There was only one way to find out. With her heart thumping, Alice went to the farmhouse to ask the farmer. She was just about to knock on the door when she heard someone whistling nearby. It was Farmer Fred. When he saw Alice, he stopped and smiled. "Hello there, Alice," he said.

"Did you have a good vacation?" Alice was so worried about Sandy that she could barely answer.

"Yes, thanks," she gulped, "but where has Sandy gone?"

"Don't worry," said the farmer. "She's safe and well in the far field. Why don't you run along and see her, but be prepared for a little surprise."

Farmer Fred smiled mysteriously, but he refused to say any more, so Alice ran off as fast as she could. By the time she got to the far field, she was feeling very hot and out of breath.

At first glance, the field looked empty, just like Sandy's paddock. "Oh, no," groaned Alice and her heart sank. She was about to burst into tears when she heard a whinnying noise.

Turning quickly, Alice spotted Sandy trotting across the field towards her. The little pony's brown coat shone in the sunshine and she shook her white mane with joy.

Alice was so pleased to see her that she flung her arms around Sandy's neck and hugged her tightly. It was only when she heard a soft neighing sound that she looked down.

Standing next to Sandy, on spindly little legs, was the cutest foal Alice had ever seen. Just like Sandy, it was caramel and covered all over with milky white spots that looked like little paint splodges.

The foal wobbled towards Alice and she gently stroked its nose. "What a wonderful little surprise," she said, smiling happily. Now she would have to spend even more time at Evergreen Farm helping to look after Sandy and her spotty foal.

The Secret Door

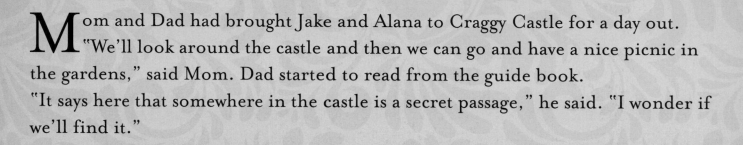

Mom and Dad had brought Jake and Alana to Craggy Castle for a day out. "We'll look around the castle and then we can go and have a nice picnic in the gardens," said Mom. Dad started to read from the guide book. "It says here that somewhere in the castle is a secret passage," he said. "I wonder if we'll find it."

Mom, Dad and Jake stopped to look at a huge picture. Reading from the guide book again, Dad said, "Legend has it that long ago, a fire-breathing dragon scared the people of the castle. It roared and rumbled, day and night."

Across the hallway, Alana was looking at a tapestry that hung on the wall. It showed an old castle, with rolling hills behind it. "That looks interesting," she thought. Suddenly, Alana heard a strange noise. She leaned in closer to the tapestry and listened carefully. Then, Alana heard it again. It was a deep rumble and seemed to be coming from behind the tapestry. Alana took hold of the edge of the fabric. Peeling it back, she discovered an old-looking door. "I wonder if this leads to the secret passage," thought Alana, opening the door and slipping past it.

Alana gasped in amazement as she stepped into a beautiful garden courtyard. Sitting in the garden was a princess wearing a long, velvet dress and had a sparkling tiara on her head. She didn't look very happy, but when she spotted Alana she sat up and smiled. "Thank goodness you're here," she said, as she jumped down from her seat. "Did the king send you to get rid of the dragon?" "No, sorry," said Alana, "but I'll help if I can."

The princess told Alana all about the dragon. "He growls and roars all day and all night," she said. "Everyone in the castle is terrified." In the distance was a loud rumble, followed by a noisy growl. "That's him now," said the princess, as she pointed up towards a tall mountain.

Alana could see a huge, scaly dragon flying down from the mountain and coming towards them. Plumes of smoke puffed out of his nose and his long tail lashed from side to side.

As the dragon flew closer, Alana noticed that the noise wasn't a roar, but a rumble. "It's coming from his stomach," she said. "He must be hungry!" Alana took off her backpack and set it down beside her. Then, she opened it and took out a packet of sandwiches from her lunch box. Bravely, she held one up for the dragon.

The dragon took the sandwich gently from Alana's hand and swallowed it down in one gulp. Then, he ate another and another until all of her lunch was gone. "We need more food," said Alana. So, the princess sent orders to the castle kitchen and the cook made a big pot of stew.

Alana and the princess carried the pot to the top of the tallest tower. Then, they lowered it carefully over the edge. The hungry dragon stuck his nose in the pot and slurped up all the stew. When he had finished, he gave a small burp and flew away.

The princess was so pleased the dragon had gone that she wanted to hold a special banquet to celebrate. "You will be my guest of honour," she said to Alana. "You are much braver than all the knights in the castle."

"That's very kind of you," said Alana, "but I'm afraid I can't stay. I have to get back to my family." Alana said goodbye to the princess and carefully opened the secret door. Glancing round to make sure no one was watching, Alana gave a final wave and crept through the doorway.

Back in the corridor, she was just about to go and find Mom, Dad and Jake when they appeared from around the corner.

As they all headed back towards the exit, they passed the tapestry with the secret door behind it. Alana smiled as she walked by, thinking of her adventure.

Suddenly, she stopped. The tapestry had changed. Instead of just showing the castle and hills, it showed the dragon, too. He looked full with a big, fat stomach. Alana stared closely at the castle and could just make out two tiny figures, on top of the tallest tower. They were pulling an empty stew pot back up the side of the castle. "That must be the princess and me," she thought, smiling.

Alana carried on along the corridor with her family. "So, has everyone had fun? What shall we do now?" asked Dad. Suddenly, there was a low, growling sound.

"What's that noise?" Mom asked, looking around.

"It's my stomach rumbling," admitted Alana. "It must be time for lunch."

As they headed out of the castle, Alana whispered to her brother,

"If you share your sandwiches with me, I'll tell you an amazing story."

"You're on!" said Jake and they set off for the castle gardens to eat their picnic.

The Missing Candy

Sophie loved to play pretend. If she wasn't a mermaid, she was a princess and if she wasn't a princess, she was a fairy. One day, Sophie decided to be a candy store owner. She laid out a rug in the garden and made an 'open and closed' sign, which she placed on top of the rug. "Now I need some bowls to fill with candy," she said to herself.

Sophie ran into the kitchen, where Mom was baking a cake. "Can I have some plastic bowls for my candy store, Mom?" she asked.
"Of course," said Mom with a smile.

Sophie took the plastic bowls and ran back into the garden. She laid them down and filled them with different candies, fudge, bon-bons and lollipops. They looked just as tasty as the ones in a real candy store. "Now, I just need my toy till and I'll be ready to open the store. I wonder who my first customer will be?" she thought, as she skipped off to fetch the till from her bedroom.

OPEN

When Sophie got back to the garden, she was surprised to see that two of the bowls were empty. "That's strange," she said. "Where have the candies gone?" Sophie searched all over, but couldn't find them. "Maybe I didn't fill those bowls up," she thought to herself, puzzled. Sophie refilled the bowls, making sure she checked they were all full. "Silly me, I've forgotten my play money, I'll need that for my store, too," she said, running back into the house.

When Sophie came back out, more candies were gone. "Oh, no!" she gasped. "Someone is taking my candy. I'm going to play detective and find out who!"

The Missing Candy

Sophie went into the kitchen, where Mom was still baking. She grabbed a notepad from the table. "Have you been out in the garden?" Sophie asked, ready to write down any clues in her detective's notepad. Sophie's mom stopped stirring the cake mixture and looked thoughtful.

"Let me see," she said. "No, I've been busy in the kitchen all afternoon." Sophie nodded and made a note in her pad.

"Where's Tommy? I bet he's been outside," Sophie asked. Sophie's little brother, Tommy, was always getting up to mischief.

"I'm not sure, he's here somewhere," said Mom. "Go and ask Dad about your missing candy, instead."

Sophie's dad was watching soccer in the front room. His team had just scored and Sophie was nearly deafened by his loud cheers. Even Monty the dog was wagging his tail, as the soccer players ran round the pitch congratulating each other. Sophie took one look at her dad, lounging on the sofa and thought, "It couldn't have been him, he wouldn't miss any of the match." Mom always said Dad wouldn't budge while the soccer was on, especially when his team was playing. Sophie decided not to disturb him. Tip-toeing out of the room, she left her dad yelling at the TV.

Feeling puzzled, Sophie wandered out into the garden. "I don't think I'll ever solve this mystery," she thought, "so I might as well finish setting up the candy store." If she tipped some of the candies that were left into the empty bowls, then she could still play her game.

As Sophie got closer to the picnic rug, she could see that something was wrong. Running the last few steps, Sophie stopped and stared. This time, nearly all the candies had gone! Only a couple were left lying in one of the bowls and a few were scattered across the rug. "That does it!" said Sophie, firmly.

Sophie was determined to get to the bottom of the mystery of the missing candy. She dashed indoors and grabbed a magnifying glass, then ran back outside and searched the scene of the crime for clues, but there was no hint of who had taken them. "There's only one way to know who it is for sure," she thought. "I'll have to catch them in the act."

Climbing up into the tree house, she settled down to keep watch over the bowls. "Whoever it is will be bound to come back for the last few candies," she thought. Sophie covered herself with a blanket so that no one could see her and laid in wait for the candy crook.

The Missing Candy

Tommy ran round the house shouting that the candy store was open in the garden. "Have you got any fudge?" asked Mom, handing over a pile of play money.

"Of course," said Sophie, counting out the change. "We've got every kind of candy in our store."

It was lots of fun running the candy store, but Sophie had to admit that investigating the mystery of the missing candies had been even more fun. "I think I would like to be a detective when I grow up," she announced, picking out a buttery toffee and popping it in her mouth. "I wonder what my next case will be."

The Wrong Wand

One morning, Fairy Lola was feeling hungry, so she decided to magic up some chocolate cupcakes. She said the magic spell and waved her wand. Instead of making a pile of delicious cakes appear, her wand shot out a puff of black smoke and broke in half. Lola looked at the broken wand dangling from her hand and sighed. "Oh, dear, now I'll have to go to Fairy Wanda's store and buy a new one," she said.

Lola fluttered straight to the store, but it was very busy. Long queues of customers were waiting to be served and Wanda was darting from shelf to shelf collecting the wands. While Lola waited for her turn, she spotted the perfect wand. It was shiny and pink with purple swirls all over it. She was just thinking how pretty it would look with her new dress, when Wanda picked it up and handed it to another fairy. "Never mind," thought Fairy Lola. "There are lots of other lovely wands."

One by one, the wands were sold. By the time Lola got to the front of the queue, there was only one wand left. It was brown and stubby with knobbly bits all over it. "What a boring wand," complained Lola.

The Wrong Wand

On the way home, Lola decided to try out her new wand. She pointed it at a toadstool and said, "Alacazo, make it grow!" She waited for a moment, but nothing happened. Fairy Lola didn't notice that the toadstool behind her had suddenly grown very large. She didn't hear the surprised yelp of the little elf who was sitting on top of it, either. "This wand is no good," thought Lola and she decided to take it back to the shop the very next day.

"Wait," called the elf, as he tried to scramble down from the huge toadstool, but Fairy Lola had gone.

A little further along the path, Lola came across a patch of big, bright, yellow flowers. "Perhaps I'll give the wand another go," she said, pointing it at one of the flowers. "Alacazink, make it shrink!" she said, waving the wand. The yellow flower waved gently in the breeze, but it did not change size.

Lola didn't see the flower behind her suddenly shrinking down, or hear the muffled buzz as a bee got trapped inside its tiny petals. Luckily, the elf had climbed down from the giant toadstool and arrived just in time to rescue the poor bee. "Stop!" cried the elf and the bee together, but Fairy Lola didn't hear them.

The little elf and the bee set off after Lola, but the fairy was too fast and they couldn't catch up with her. "I knew this wand wasn't right for me," she grumbled to herself as she strode along. Fairy Lola was so busy complaining about the new wand, that she almost walked into a tree.

Feeling cross, she aimed the wand at the trunk and said a spell to turn it into a pumpkin. The tree in front of her stayed where it was. However, the old oak tree that was behind her transformed in a golden flash, leaving a startled squirrel floating in mid-air and two pumpkins on the ground.

The elf and the bee had just caught up with Lola. They threw themselves forwards and managed to catch the falling squirrel before it hit the ground. Then, the elf, the bee and the squirrel each took a deep breath and shouted as loudly as they could, "LITTLE FAIRY, PLEASE STOP!"

At last, Fairy Lola heard them and turned around to see what all the fuss was about. "Your wand is wrong," panted the exhausted elf.
"I know, it doesn't even work," agreed Lola. "I'm taking it back to Wanda's store tomorrow."
"No," cried the elf. "You're holding it the wrong way round!"

88

The Wrong Wand

The little elf told Lola about the giant toadstool, the tiny flower and the disappearing tree. "They were behind you," he explained, "because your wand was pointing in the wrong direction."

The little fairy looked at the new wand and then opened the book of instructions to read the first page. "I'm so sorry," she gasped. "I know how I can make it up to you." She turned her wand around and gave it a swish. A magnificent picnic appeared with cupcakes, strawberries and fruit for them all to share. "I think this is the right wand for me after all," smiled Fairy Lola and her new friends all agreed.

Abigail's Perfect Pet

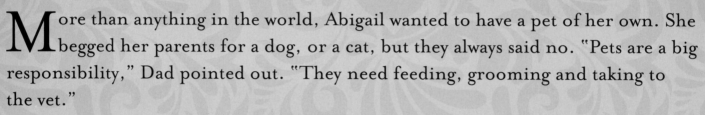

More than anything in the world, Abigail wanted to have a pet of her own. She begged her parents for a dog, or a cat, but they always said no. "Pets are a big responsibility," Dad pointed out. "They need feeding, grooming and taking to the vet."

"You're not quite big enough to look after a pet just yet," added Mom. "Maybe when you're a bit older."

Then one day, Mom and Abigail were walking home from the shops and bumped into their neighbor, Mrs Brown. She had been out for a walk with her dog, Digby.

"I'm afraid Digby didn't get much exercise today," said Mrs Brown, pointing to her bandaged leg. "I've hurt my ankle and I can't walk very far." Mom looked at Abigail, who was making a fuss of Digby. He wagged his tail happily as Abigail stroked the soft, fluffy fur on his tummy.

"I think I know someone who'd be happy to walk Digby for you," she said, smiling. "Abigail loves dogs."

"It would be a great help if you could take him for a good walk," Mrs Brown said to Abigail. "I'm sure Digby would love it, too."

So, the next day, Abigail set off for the park holding tightly onto Digby's lead.

"You were right, Mom," said Abigail. "Looking after a pet is hard work.
I think I'll wait until I'm a bit older before I ask for one again."
"That's very grown up of you," said Mom and she gave Abigail a big hug.

A few days later, Mom and Dad told Abigail they had a special surprise for her.
When she came into the room, Abigail was amazed to find a glass bowl with
a shiny, little goldfish swimming around inside. "This is for you," said Dad.
"A goldfish is much easier to look after than a dog."
"We know you'll take good care of him," added Mom.
Abigail peered into the bowl and smiled. "He's the perfect pet," she said.

The Spoilt Princess

There once was a princess who had a magical fairy godmother. Whenever she wanted something, the princess would summon the fairy godmother and order her to magic it up, but she never said "please" or "thank you". "I want a thousand cupcakes," she demanded, one day.

"Yes, dear," said the fairy godmother, waving her wand. There was a bright flash and a huge pile of cupcakes appeared. The princess picked up a cake with little, pink sugar flowers on it and took a bite. "I'm bored of cupcakes now," she said, tossing it aside.

Next, the princess decided that she wanted a pet. "I don't want something boring," she told the fairy godmother. "I want a dragon."

"Right away, dear," said the fairy godmother, muttering the magic spell. A huge, purple dragon appeared, shooting flames from its scaly nose. "Watch out!" shouted the king. "It's going to burn down the palace."

"Make it go away!" screamed the princess.

The fairy godmother waved her wand again and the dragon's flames were gone, leaving only black puffs of smoke coming from his nose. The princess looked down at her dress. It was covered in sooty, black smudges. "Now I need a new dress," she said. The princess looked at her fairy godmother and crossed her arms. "Magic me up a pretty dress," she ordered.

With a swish of her wand, the fairy godmother conjured up a beautiful, bright yellow gown. It was covered in sequins that sparkled like the stars. The princess was about to say that it was the prettiest dress she had ever seen, but just then she spotted a flower bed full of pink roses. "I wanted a pink dress," she complained. "Yellow is horrible!" The poor fairy godmother was beginning to feel tired from doing so much magic, but she gave her wand a flick and turned the yellow dress into a pink one.

The pink dress was as delicate and pretty as a petal, but the princess barely glanced at it. She was too busy watching a bluebird hopping about on the lawn. "I don't want pink anymore," she said. "Change the dress to blue."

With a sigh, the fairy godmother raised her wand. She was in the middle of casting her spell when the princess caught sight of the strawberry patch. "Red dress!" she cried. Then a bumblebee buzzed by. "Stripy dress!" she shouted. Finally a rainbow butterfly fluttered through the palace garden. "I want a dress with every single shade in it," demanded the princess.

The dress flashed and fizzed as it changed from one shade to another.
One moment it was sky blue, the next it was bright red, then stripy, then it was
rainbow-patterned. The princess looked down at her gown in alarm.
"What's happening?" she cried.

Before the fairy godmother could answer, there was a loud POP and the dress
began to fall to pieces. The fairy godmother flopped down into a garden chair,
the broken wand hanging from her hand. There was a big hole scorched in her
cloak. "My wand has burned out," she explained, weakly. "It was too much magic."

The fairy godmother was so worn out that she fell fast asleep and was soon snoring loudly. Looking at her red face and frazzled hair, the princess realised how hard the fairy godmother had tried to make her happy. "She has always been so kind to me and I have been very selfish," she thought. "Now her wand has broken and her cloak is ruined."

The princess didn't know how to mend a magic wand, but she took a close look at the burned cloak. "I think I can do something special to show her how sorry I am," she said to herself. Picking up all the pieces of her dress, the princess ran into the palace and dropped them in a pile next to her sewing machine.

One by one, she stitched the different scraps of material together. She worked as fast as she could and soon she had made a beautiful new cloak.

When the fairy godmother woke up, she was amazed to find the princess hard at work in the sewing room. She was even more surprised when she saw what the princess had made. "It's wonderful!" exclaimed the fairy, putting on the patchwork cloak and twirling round. "It's so much prettier than my old one."

"I'm sorry for being selfish and spoiled," said the princess. "I will wear one of my old dresses and if I want a new one, I can make it myself."

The fairy godmother was so pleased with the princess that she quickly mended her worn-out wand. Then, she swung it with a swoosh and made a twinkling tiara appear. "Now we can both wear something bright and beautiful," she said to the princess, placing the tiara gently on her head. The princess smiled a big smile and said thank you to her magical fairy godmother for the very first time.

Bridesmaid Blues

"I've got a lovely surprise for you," Tara's mom said to her one day. "You're going to be a bridesmaid at Aunt Helen's wedding."

Tara stopped kicking her ball round the garden and frowned. "I don't want to be a bridesmaid though," she complained. "I don't like frilly dresses or silly shoes."

"I'm sure Aunt Helen will choose a lovely dress and very nice shoes for you," said her mom.

Tara had seen what her friends had worn when they were bridesmaids. Their dresses were covered in beads and bows and their shoes were like something a fairy would wear to a ball. She didn't want to look like a fairy. Tara was a tomboy and liked to wear comfy jeans and trainers, not horrible, girly, pink dresses. "Will I have to carry a bunch of flowers and have my hair done up like a princess?" she asked, wrinkling her nose in disgust. Tara's mom sighed. "That would be a dream come true for most girls," she pointed out.

Tara kicked the ball into the goal. She would much rather play soccer with her friends, or roller-skate round the park than spend a whole day being a bridesmaid.

Later that day, Tara's mom climbed up into the attic and brought down an old bridesmaid dress for her to try on. Tara looked at it in horror. The dress was made from shiny, pink material with puffed-out sleeves and had a big bow tied at the back.

"Your Aunt Helen looked lovely wearing this at my wedding," said Mom, staring dreamily at the dress. "I don't know why she didn't want to keep it." Reluctantly, Tara climbed into the dress. It was too big for her and felt scratchy against her skin. "You look like a giant marshmallow," said Tara's brother, laughing so hard that he got the hiccups.

Bridesmaid Blues

That evening, Aunt Helen came round to talk about the wedding. Tara just sat there smiling, politely. When Tara's mom went into the kitchen to make a drink, Aunt Helen leaned over to Tara. "What's wrong?" she asked.

"I do want to come to your wedding," replied Tara, "but I don't want to wear a horrible dress." Aunt Helen chuckled.

"Like the one I had to wear to your mom's wedding you mean? I hated it!" she said, laughing. "Didn't your mom tell you what a fuss I made about wearing that dress?" Tara shook her head.

"She must have forgotten," said Tara, shrugging her shoulders.

"Well, I've got some cool ideas for your outfit," said Aunt Helen, as she smiled mysteriously.

The next day, Aunt Helen took Tara shopping for her bridesmaid dress. Tara couldn't wait to find out what her aunt was planning, but when they got to the shop it was full of frilly gowns and fancy shoes. "Oh, no," thought Tara. "I don't want to wear any of these outfits."

Aunt Helen had a word with the shop assistant who disappeared into the back of the shop. When she came back, she was carrying a long, flowing dress that Tara thought looked cool. She tried the dress on and it fitted perfectly. "I suppose it is quite nice for a dress. At least there are no bows or frills on it," said Tara, smiling a little.

Bridesmaid Blues

As soon as she got home, Tara dashed straight upstairs to tell her mom all about the bridesmaid dress. Bursting into the room, she was surprised to find her brother trying on his outfit for the wedding. It was a smart suit with a waistcoat, bow tie and top hat.

Tara couldn't help giggling when she saw how uncomfortable her brother looked. He wriggled and complained while Mom did up his bow tie. "It's too stiff and it's so scratchy," he moaned, "and it makes me look silly."
"Nonsense," said Mom. "I think you look very handsome." Tara thought about how he had teased her the day before and she smiled. "Who looks silly now," she thought.

When the big day arrived, Tara went to Aunt Helen's house to help her get ready. Then, they climbed into the shiny wedding car. As they drove through the town to the church, Tara waved like a princess at everyone they passed in the street. She had to admit there were some good things about being a bridesmaid.

Outside the church, the rest of the family were waiting for them. Tara's mom was holding a box of confetti and her brother was fidgeting and tugging at his bow tie. Aunt Helen stepped out of the car and Tara passed her a bouquet of blue flowers. Then, she added the finishing touches to her own special outfit.

Bridesmaid Blues

Everyone turned to watch as Aunt Helen walked slowly along the path towards the church. She looked beautiful in her long, white dress and twinkling tiara. Mom was throwing confetti into the air, but Tara's brother was staring at his sister as she glided along behind the bride. "Look at Tara, Mom," he said. "She looks like she's flying!"

"Oh, doesn't she look lovely in that dress," smiled Mom. "I wonder what shoes Aunt Helen chose for her." Tara turned and winked at her brother as she floated past. It was a good job the bridesmaid dress was long enough to cover her roller skates!

Princess Arabella's New Kite

It was a windy day and Princess Arabella was very excited. She grabbed her new kite and ran out into the palace garden. The kite was pink with lots of bright bows hanging from the bottom. The princess had been waiting ages for a windy day so she could play with it. "I can't wait to see how high it can fly," she said, as she unravelled the string. "I'm sure it will go higher than the palace tower."

At that moment, Arabella's little sister, Princess Jennifer, skipped out into the garden. "Can I play with the kite, too?" she asked.
"No, you're too small," snapped Princess Arabella, snatching up the kite and marching off to the other end of the garden.

Princess Jennifer sat down on the garden bench and watched, sadly, as her sister tried to launch the pink kite into the sky. It took several tries, but eventually Princess Arabella managed to get the kite up into the air. It swooped and soared in the breeze, the bow-covered string swirling along behind it. Princess Arabella smiled as she tugged at the kite's string, making it dip and dance, but the kite pulled harder and harder until she could only just hold onto it.

Whoosh! A strong gust of wind caught hold of the kite and sent it shooting straight into the prickly branches at the top of a bramble bush. "Oh, no!" cried Princess Arabella. She tugged at the kite's string to try and pull it free, but it was stuck fast on the spiky thorns.

"Do you need any help?" said a voice from behind Arabella. Princess Jennifer stood, looking up at Princess Arabella. "No thanks, I can do it on my own," said Arabella. She stood on her tiptoes and just managed to grasp the end of the kite with her fingertips. "Got it," she sighed with relief.

Princess Arabella climbed down and started to fly her kite again. It looked amazing as it looped through the air. The wind blustered and blew and Arabella struggled to hold on to the kite's string. "Shall I help you to hold it so it doesn't blow away again?" said Princess Jennifer, who was watching Arabella struggle with the strong wind.

"No thanks, I can manage," said Arabella. She was determined not to let go.

Suddenly, there was a loud SNAP! The string broke and the kite soared away.

Princess Arabella watched her kite disappear into the distance and started to cry. "Now it's gone forever," she said, as she wiped the tears from her cheek.

Princess Jennifer saw how upset her sister was and went over to see if she was okay. "Never mind," said Princess Jennifer, putting an arm around her big sister, "maybe we can make a better kite together." Princess Arabella wiped her eyes. "That's a good idea," she sniffed.

The two sisters collected everything they needed and started making a new kite. They glued on shiny sequins and painted pretty patterns onto it. They attached a long, thick piece of string and tied an extra-strong knot in the end.

The next day, the sisters ran out into the garden. They sent the heart-shaped kite into the air and held on tight to their strings, as it soared straight up and floated on the breeze. As it flew, the long streamers waved like ribbons in the wind and the sequins dazzled in the sunlight. "It's much more fun flying together," said Princess Arabella. "I'm sorry I wouldn't let you play before," she said.
"It's okay," said Princess Jennifer, "Now we have an amazing kite to share with each other," she said smiling.

Slumber Party Surprise

Lauren loved staying over at her friends' houses when they had slumber parties. It was so much fun staying up late, giggling and gossiping as they snuggled up in their sleeping bags. Lauren decided that she wanted to hold a slumber party of her own.

There was just one problem, Lauren's little sister, Molly. The two girls shared a bedroom and Mom thought a slumber party would be too noisy. "All that chattering will keep Molly awake," she said. "You know how grouchy your little sister gets when she's tired."

"Please, Mom," Lauren argued. "Everyone else is allowed to have one, why can't I?"

"I've got an idea," said Mom. "Gran's coming over soon, why don't you ask if you can have a slumber party at her house?"

Lauren wasn't sure. She loved Gran, who was cheerful and cuddly and made the best chocolate brownies ever, but a slumber party at her house might be a bit, old-fashioned. "What if Gran gets us to do knitting? Or shows everyone my baby photos?" said Lauren. Mom laughed.

"Don't worry, Gran organized brilliant parties when I was your age. You might be in for a nice surprise!"

So, when Gran came over, Lauren asked her about the slumber party. "Oh, yes!" said Gran, clapping her hands together. "I haven't had a slumber party for years."

On the night of the slumber party, Lauren began to feel more and more worried. What if Gran played her old records or made them watch soaps on TV? Lauren packed her pajamas and rolled up her sleeping bag, but she wasn't looking forward to the slumber party very much at all.

Mom dropped her round at Gran's house early so she could help get everything organized and ready. As she walked into the front room, she couldn't believe her eyes. There were piles of delicious party food and a super-scrummy chocolate fountain. Gran had even changed her front room into a disco, complete with disco lights.

"I love a good party," said Gran, passing Lauren some balloons to blow up.
"Everything looks amazing," gasped Lauren, between puffs on the balloon.
"I can't wait for the slumber party to start."

As soon as Lauren's friends, Sally and Charlotte arrived, Gran got them to play
silly games with the balloons until they were laughing so much they could barely
stand up. Then, she suggested dressing up as pop stars and making up their
own dance routine. Sally and Charlotte chose cool outfits while Gran put on
some music. Lauren was relieved to hear that it was the latest hits and not Gran's
old record collection. The disco lights twinkled and flashed as the girls danced to
the beat and sang into their pretend microphones.

Next, Gran gave Lauren and her friends a movie-star makeover. First, she braided and styled Charlotte's hair into the most beautiful designs, then she painted Sally and Lauren's nails in every shade of the rainbow. "Who would like some face paint on?" Gran asked the girls.

"Me!" shouted the girls at once. So, Gran carefully painted little stars, hearts and butterflies on their faces.

Finally, Gran brought out lots of sparkly dresses, feather boas and big hats for the girls to dress up in. Lauren, Charlotte and Sally strutted up and down on the rug, pretending it was a red carpet and they were movie stars going to a premiere.

Soon, it was time for Lauren and her friends to get into their pajamas and snuggle up for a spooky story. Gran made up some mugs of steaming hot chocolate with swirls of cream and mini marshmallows floating on the top.

Then, she settled down on the sofa to read them a spine-tingling tale about a ghostly pirate ship. The girls sipped their drinks and listened intently as Gran told the creepy story. When she got to the end, Lauren shivered. "I'm glad I'm not on that ship," she said, pulling the fluffy blanket closer around her. "It's much cozier here."

Lauren and her friends chatted about all the fun things they had done at the slumber party while they finished drinking their hot chocolate. "That chocolate fountain was so yummy," said Charlotte, popping a mini marshmallow into her mouth.

"Oh, I liked the makeover best," said Sally, as she patted her new hairstyle.

"I never knew Gran was so good at dancing," smiled Lauren, remembering her Gran's funky moves on the dance floor. Gran waved the book of spooky stories in the air.

"I'll just go and put this away," she said and popped out of the room.

124

When Gran came back a few moments later, she was carrying a tray full of candy treats and tasty snacks. "Surprise!" she said, peering round the huge pile of candy and cupcakes. "Who's ready for a mega midnight feast?"

No one answered. Instead there was a soft snoring noise. Lauren and her friends had fallen fast asleep and were snoozing peacefully on the sofa. Gran looked at them curled up together and smiled. "Well it looks like I can still hold the best slumber parties," she said to herself, as she settled down under a fluffy blanket to enjoy the midnight feast.

The Fairy Night Light

"What a wonderful day," sighed Faye the fairy, as she said goodbye to the Enchanted Forest and set off home with her family. Faye felt tired and happy after playing chase with the squirrels and splashing about in the silvery pond. She giggled when she thought of how the little fish had tickled her toes. Faye waved to the unicorns as she skipped along and they neighed back at her, happily. Beautiful little butterflies fluttered past and the birds sang as they settled down in the branches to rest. The sky was turning pink and orange and the sun was slowly sinking behind the trees.

"Look at that beautiful sunset," said Mom. Dad, Mom and Faye all stopped to watch, but Faye was staring at the ground. Shadows seemed to be creeping out from under the plants and trees. They stretched across the woodland floor, making the forest a darker and colder place. Faye shivered and took hold of Dad's hand.
"I don't like the dark," she whispered. "It's scary."

"There's no need to be afraid of the dark," said Dad, giving Faye's hand a soft, little squeeze. "When the sun goes down, you can see all kinds of things you can't see in the daylight."

"Like what?" wondered Faye, curiously. "Surely you can see less in the dark, not even more." Dad laughed.

"Well, take a good look around you and see what you can see here," he said.

Faye looked either side of the path. The bushes were covered in bright little sparks. "Those are glow-worms," explained Dad. "Don't forget to look up, too." Dipping and darting through the air were hundreds of fireflies. They twinkled and sparkled, as they flitted about, lighting up the night sky.

Then, Dad showed Faye the moonbeam flowers that grew deep within the Enchanted Forest. "Their petals hold the light, then they glow brightly all through the night," he explained.

Faye thought the flowers were beautiful. "They look like little stars that have fallen from the sky," she said.
"Let's pick some to take home with us," suggested Mom. So, they all began to gather bunches of the bright blooms. Soon, they had armfuls of pretty flowers.
"Time to go," said Dad and he told Faye and her sister how they could use the stars to find their way home.

Mom, Dad and Faye followed the sparkling stars, all the way back to their cozy little house. Faye was pleased to be home, safe and warm with a nice hot supper, but she couldn't help gazing out of the window at the golden moon and starry sky. "Come on, everyone," called Mom. "You can all help me make a moonbeam flower decoration to hang up."

Mom piled the flowers on the table and used spider's silk to weave them into a pretty pattern. They worked together to turn the blooms into a wonderful mobile that shone softly. When it was time for bed, Dad hung it up in Faye's room. "To remind you of how beautiful the night can be," he said, as he smiled at her.

Faye gave her dad a hug as he tucked her in. "Thank you for showing me all the pretty night-time things," she said. "I'm not afraid of the dark anymore." Faye thought about the fireflies and the glow-worms, the moon and the stars. If it wasn't for the dark night, she wouldn't be able to see any of them. "Nothing that pretty can be scary," she decided.

Dad kissed her goodnight and turned off her lamp. The decoration gave a warm glow like a flowery night light. "I may not be scared of the dark anymore," thought Faye, "but I think I'll keep the moonbeam flowers in my bedroom for a while, just in case!"

131

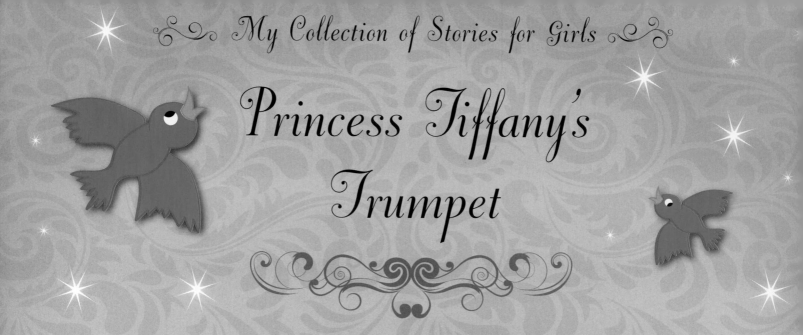

Princess Tiffany's Trumpet

There was a terrible noise coming from the pink palace on top of the hill. The royal unicorns galloped away in fright. Even the dragon who lived in the cave under the hill put his paws over his ears.

Princess Tiffany was playing her trumpet. The princess loved to make music and was always humming or singing as she played in the palace or skipped round the gardens. She played the piano, the harp and even the electric guitar, but the instrument she liked the most was the trumpet. The trouble was, she wasn't very good at playing it. "If I keep trying, I'm sure to get better," she told herself. Then, she took a deep breath, raised the trumpet to her lips and blew as hard as she could. PAAARP! The palace walls shook and the crystal chandeliers tinkled.

Outside, the gardener stuffed carrots in his ears and in the kitchen, the chef pulled his tall, white hat down over his head, but none of it helped. Nothing could block out the awful noise. "I think that sounds much better," decided Princess Tiffany. "I wonder where Mom is. I bet she'd love to hear me play." Carrying her trumpet in one hand and a book of music in the other, Princess Tiffany set off to search for the queen.

The queen was relaxing on her throne when Princess Tiffany burst through the door and blasted out a loud fanfare on her trumpet. "Aargh!" cried the queen, leaping off the throne in shock. The dreadful sound woke up the royal cat, who had been dreaming about a giant bowl of cream. Miaow! he shrieked, flying into the air, with his tail stuck out and his fur standing on end.

"That trumpet is too noisy," said the queen crossly. "Go and play in the tower so I can read in peace."
"Sorry," said Princess Tiffany and she trudged off to the tower.

Princess Tiffany climbed the spiral staircase. When she got to the top of the tower, she could hear a little tooting noise. "Dad must be playing with his train set again," sighed Princess Tiffany. "I can make a better sound than that." She drew in a deep breath of air and threw open the door, blasting out TOOT-TOOT on her trumpet.

The king was so surprised by the sound that he dropped the control box for his model train set. His little engine sped off the tracks, bounced over the model station before crashing into a bridge. "This is no place for trumpets!" cried the king, picking up the broken pieces of his engine. "Go and play outside."

Out on the lawn, Princess Tiffany's brother was painting a picture of the garden. The birds were singing and the bees hummed as they flew from flower to flower. It sounded so lovely that Princess Tiffany wanted to join in. She tried to play a melody like the beautiful birdsong, but all that came out was a harsh, honking sort of sound.

"What's making that terrible racket?" said her brother, sploshing water all over the paper. Paint ran down the picture making a blurry mess.
"It's just me playing my trumpet," explained Princess Tiffany.
"You made me jump," said her brother. "Now I've ruined my picture."

Just then, the royal gardener arrived with some beautiful flowers to plant in the garden. The prince perked up. "Ooh, they'd make an even better painting," he said, as he grabbed his brush and a clean piece of paper. "Why don't you find somewhere else to play Tiffany?"

"I don't know where to go," said Princess Tiffany, sadly.

"Don't worry," said the gardener. "I know the perfect place for you to play your trumpet." He took Princess Tiffany through the wooden gate that led into the kitchen garden. It was where he grew all the fruit and vegetables for the palace and it was surrounded by thick, brick walls.

"Those walls will stop the sound of your trumpet from disturbing anyone," explained the gardener. "Oh, thank you," said Princess Tiffany, looking around at all the leafy, green plants.

Birds of all shapes and sizes were busy pecking at the fruits and vegetables. They hopped from the berry bushes to the vegetable patch, taking no notice of the scarecrow that stood in the middle of the garden. "Perhaps I can help you, too," said the princess. She took a deep breath and blew a thunderous blast on her trumpet. Suddenly, the air was full of flapping wings as the birds shot up into the sky in fright.

Princess Tiffany's Trumpet

Princess Tiffany carried on playing until all the birds had flown away. After a while, the gardener took off his headphones and listened to her play. She was definitely getting better. When she had run out of puff, they both sat down to rest on the garden bench. "I've got a special reward for you," said the gardener and he pulled out a big bowl of sweet, juicy strawberries. "If it wasn't for you, the birds would have taken all of these and lots more. You can play your trumpet here whenever you like." Princess Tiffany picked out a plump, red strawberry and smiled. Now that she could rehearse every day, she would soon be the best trumpet player ever.

Princess Bella's First Day

It was Princess Bella's first day at royal school and she was feeling nervous as she walked through the golden gates. All around her, princes and princesses were laughing and smiling, as they played together. "I wish I had some friends," thought Bella, sadly. "What if no one talks to me all day?"

Bella didn't know anyone at the school and she felt too shy to ask any of the children to play. Instead, she wandered round the playground feeling sad and lonely. Some of the girls were singing as they skipped together, but Bella didn't know the song so she didn't stop to join in.

A bit further on, a group of boys were racing and chasing each other as they played a game of tag. Bella stepped quickly out of the way as they thundered past, putting her foot straight into a muddy puddle. Princess Bella felt her bottom lip begin to wobble and her eyes fill up with tears. She had woken up extra-early to make sure her shoes were shining brightly ready for her first day. Now, they were covered in dirt. "I don't think I like school," she thought. Just then, the bell rang. It was time to line up and go inside.

The lessons were fun and the morning flew by quickly, but Bella was not looking forward to play time. "I don't want to be all by myself again," she thought, as she walked out into the playground.

Bella was watching the other children scampering around, laughing and calling to each other, when she heard a friendly voice. "Hello, I'm Princess Wendy. Would you like to play with me?" said a kind-looking girl.
"I'm Princess Bella," she replied nervously. "I'd love to play with you." The two princesses had a game of hopscotch and by the time play time ended, Bella felt much better.

Princess Bella's First Day

At lunchtime, Princess Bella played with Princess Wendy again. They skipped and played catch, then made up a game about fairies and fluttered all around the playground. "Let's ask some more girls to join in," said Wendy. "It'll be great fun." Bella wasn't sure. What if no one else wanted to play with her? Wendy had already run off to round up some of her friends.

Soon, there was a group of girls chatting and giggling as they pretended to be fairies. Bella was right in the middle of all the fun, smiling happily. "I think I do like school after all," she said.

While Bella was playing with her new friends, she noticed a little girl sitting all alone and looking sad. "That girl looks just like I did this morning," Bella thought, as she skipped over and sat down next to the girl. "Hello, would you like to join our game?" she asked. "I'm Princess Bella."
"Yes, please," the girl said looking up and smiling shyly. "My name is Princess Paige."

As the two girls skipped off to play, Paige explained that she was new and didn't know anybody at the school. "Well, you do now," said Bella. "You know me."
"You must have been at this school for ages," said Paige. "You've got so many friends."
"I'm new, too," Princess Bella said, laughing. "Don't worry you'll soon have lots of friends to play with."

Bella took Paige over to meet Wendy and the other girls. They offered to teach
the two new princesses a skipping song. Before long, Bella and Paige were
hopping and jumping over the skipping rope, singing loudly. They had such
a lovely time, they quickly became the best of friends. "It's good to be friendly
when you meet someone new," said Bella.

"Now, we'll never be lonely at school again," said Paige.

145

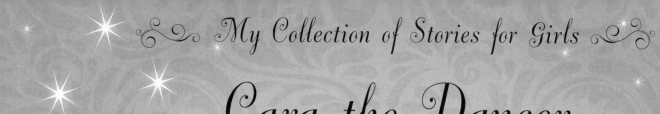

Cara the Dancer

At Miss Prim's School of Dance everyone was excited. The annual grand ballet show was less than a week away and all the girls were busy preparing. Some were practicing their dancing, others were testing out new hairstyles and Miss Prim was choosing the music. Cara as usual, was helping out by painting the sets. She loved to watch the girls dance and loved to dance herself, but she was far too shy to do it in front of an audience.

As Cara sat painting, Isabelle walked past. "Hello, Cara. That looks lovely," she said, looking at the set.
"Thank you, Isabelle," Cara replied, shyly. Isabelle was a wonderful dancer and Cara loved watching her. She was so graceful and elegant and had the lead role in this year's show. Cara dreamed of being as good a dancer as Isabelle.

A little later on, when nearly all the other girls had gone, Cara was left alone backstage. As the sound of Miss Prim's music came floating through the air, Cara began to dance. Her arms and legs began to move to the rhythm, copying the steps that she had watched a hundred times before. Her eyes closed and she happily moved from one side of the floor to the other, spinning, leaping and bounding. When the music came to an end, Cara curtsied elegantly to an imaginary audience. She had no idea that Miss Prim had been watching her the whole time.

"Bravo!" cried Miss Prim, clapping her hands in delight. Cara jumped in surprise and blushed bright red.

"I didn't know you were there, Miss Prim," she said. "I'm sorry, I'll get on with painting the scenery."

"Nonsense! You should be dancing with the other ballerinas," said Miss Prim.

"Surely I'm not good enough," whispered Cara, looking down at her feet.

"You are a very talented dancer," said Miss Prim, smiling. "You just need to believe in yourself. Keep trying and I am sure that one day, you will be the star of the show."

From that moment on, Cara followed Miss Prim's advice and practiced her dance moves each evening, until she knew the routine off by heart.

Cara the Dancer

The night before the show came, as Cara drifted off to sleep, she found herself in a wonderful dream. Cara dreamed that she was the star of the ballet, dancing on a grand stage in front of a huge audience and wasn't afraid at all. A sparkling dress glittered and flowed around her with every step. In her dream, Cara's face glowed, as she pranced and swirled to the magical music. She could still hear the crowd cheering as she woke up in her own, snug bed. "If only my dream was true," she said, sadly.

When Cara arrived at ballet the next day, she could tell straight away that something was wrong. Instead of stretching and warming up, the other dancers were huddled around Isabelle, whispering and looking worried. "Poor Isabelle has a stomach ache," explained one of the girls. "Miss Prim says she has to go home and won't be able to dance in the show."

Cara wondered how the other ballerinas would manage without her. "What will happen to the show if Isabelle can't dance?" she asked, but the girls just shrugged. "We don't know," they said. "Miss Prim is going to make an announcement."

Miss Prim strode into the room and everyone went quiet. She looked serious and Cara began to feel worried. "Isabelle can't dance in the show and we need someone to replace her, otherwise the show will have to be canceled," said Miss Prim. The ballerinas sighed, shaking their heads in disappointment.

"If only Isabelle had an understudy," said one of the girls. Cara had an idea, but she wasn't sure if she was brave enough to say anything.

Before she could suggest it, Cara heard Miss Prim say her name. Looking up, Cara realized that all the girls were looking at her. "So, Cara, would you like to be Isabelle's understudy?" repeated Miss Prim.

"Erm," said Cara, looking round at all the girls, "I could try, if you'd like me to?" Miss Prim smiled with relief.

"Let's start rehearsing straight away then," she said.

Cara and the other girls performed the routine over and over again. "I won't let the other ballerinas down," she told herself, but as the start of the show got closer, Cara began to feel nervous. Her stomach felt like it was full of butterflies. "It's normal to feel a little anxious," said Miss Prim soothingly. "Just try to enjoy yourself and you will dance beautifully."

Backstage on the night of the show, all the ballerinas were getting ready. "At last, I get to wear one of these lovely tutus," thought Cara. She put on a twinkling pink tutu, a pair of silk ballet shoes and a beautiful, sparkling tiara, then walked toward the stage.

Cara the Dancer

Cara took up her position and bravely waited for the show to start. The curtain lifted and suddenly she could see the audience clapping and smiling. Cara smiled back and, as the music played and the lights shone brightly, she started to dance.

It felt wonderful to be gliding round the stage, sweeping up her arms and stretching out her legs. "It's just like my dream," thought Cara, forgetting all about her nerves. She took several quick, light steps and then, with a giant leap, Cara flew into the air for her big move. The audience gasped as she soared upwards and cheered loudly when she landed perfectly.

Cara and the ballerinas whirled and twirled around the stage, but all too soon the show came to an end. "I wish I could carry on dancing all night long," thought Cara, as the audience applauded and tossed flowers at her feet.

At last, the curtain came down and all the other dancers gathered round Cara. They were so pleased that she had stepped in to save the show and everyone thought she had danced beautifully. "I can't believe you learned the part so quickly," said one of the girls.

"I already knew the routine," admitted Cara. "Finally, I don't have to worry about being shy in front of people. Dancing on the stage isn't as scary as I thought."

Miss Prim congratulated all the dancers on a wonderful performance. Then, she turned to Cara. "So, how does it feel to be a real ballerina?" Cara thought for a moment. She looked around her at the stage, the other dancers and her own sparkling tutu. Then, with a big, beaming smile, she said, "It feels like a dream come true!"

The Rainbow Fairy

Roxie was thrilled when the fairy queen gave her a special job. She was going to be the new rainbow fairy. It was up to her to create beautiful, shimmering rainbows that arched across the sky.

There was just one small problem. Roxie didn't know how to create a rainbow. She tried flicking her wand back and forth, but that just made some dull fog appear. "That doesn't look anything like a rainbow," said Roxie. So, she twirled her wand in circles. Bright sparkles flew out of the end. They were red, orange, yellow, green, blue, indigo and violet. "Phew!" Roxie sighed. "At least these are right, but how do I make them into a rainbow?"

She decided to try casting a spell. "Green swirl and yellow flow, turn into a bright rainbow," Roxie chanted. Nothing happened, so after a while she sprinkled some fairy dust around. "Aatchoo!" The dust got up Roxie's nose and made her sneeze, but it didn't make a rainbow. Roxie was beginning to feel a bit worried. What would the fairy queen say when she heard that her new rainbow fairy couldn't make a rainbow?

"I need some help," thought Roxie and she fluttered away to find her friends. She hadn't flown far when she came across Flutterwing, the wind fairy. She was busy blowing the white fluffy seeds off a dandelion head. Each tiny tap of her wand made a little puff of air waft over the flower. "Please can you help me?" begged Roxie. She told Flutterwing how she had tried to make a rainbow. "First you need a gust of wind," said Flutterwing, waggling her wand. Leaves began to fly from the trees and fluffy white clouds rolled across the sky. "Now, go and find Droplet, the rain fairy."

So, Roxie set off towards the waterfall where Droplet lived. As she got closer, she could hear the whoosh of water tumbling down into the blue pool.

Droplet was sitting on a rock, dipping her toes in the cool water. When Roxie explained why she was visiting, Droplet laughed. "I can help you," she said and with a wave of her wand, Droplet made a shower of glittering raindrops fall from the clouds. "I don't understand," said Roxie, with a puzzled look on her face. "You will," said Droplet, "but first you need to go and see Sunbeam, the sun fairy."

Roxie felt confused as she soared into the sky. How could the wind and rain help her make a beautiful rainbow? "Now I'm soaking wet and getting blown all over the place," she complained. "Maybe Sunbeam can explain."

She made her way to the sun fairy's house on top of the big hill. Sunbeam was busy watering her sunflowers, but when she heard what Roxie had to say, she fetched her wand.

The two fairies stood on the edge of the hill and Sunbeam swung her wand through the air. Golden sunlight beamed down on the hillside, making the raindrops sparkle and shine.

The Rainbow Fairy

"Your turn," said Sunbeam and Roxie swished her wand. There was a flash of magic and then a rainbow began to rise up from behind the hills. "It's beautiful," gasped Roxie. The rainbow stretched up through the sky before arching back down to the ground.

"To make a rainbow, you need the wind to bring some rain clouds," explained Sunbeam. "Then, all it takes is some rain, sunshine and a bit of magic." "What I needed most of all was my friends," said Roxie. "It takes teamwork to make a rainbow." She smiled happily. Not only did Roxie have a brilliant job, she also had three fantastic friends to share it with.

Pop to the Top

Sadie and her friends were in her room, chatting and listening to music, when suddenly Sadie dashed over to the radio and turned it up. "Shhh," she said, waving to hush her friends. "I want to hear this."

"Has your band got what it takes to make it to the top?" said the DJ. "Then rock along to the Stars of Pop competition and show us your star quality." Sadie looked round with a big grin on her face.

"We have got to enter that contest," she said, but her friends didn't look so sure.

"We haven't got a band, Sadie," pointed out Milly.

"We don't know how to play any songs," added Charlotte.

"Or have any outfits to wear on stage," agreed Kayla.

Sadie was not going to be put off so easily though. She'd wanted to be a pop star since she was tiny and this was her big chance. "We all play instruments," she said. "Let's start a band. It'll be easy to learn a couple of songs." So, her friends popped home to collect their instruments and they agreed to meet in Sadie's garage for their first rehearsal.

A couple of hours later, Sadie was beginning to wonder if starting a band was such a good idea. Her friends played the violin, flute and trombone. They didn't look much like a pop group and when they played together, they sounded dreadful.

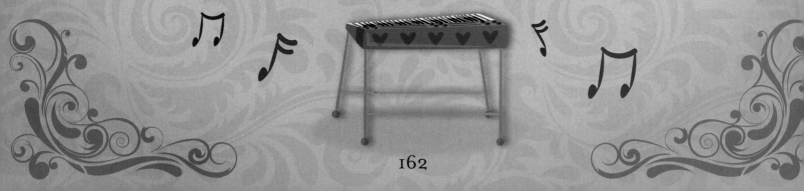

"I know what will make us sound better," said Sadie. "We need some backing music." She pressed a few buttons on her keyboard until it started playing a steady, pounding beat. Then, she mixed in some funky sound effects. The girls picked up their instruments and started playing again. Sadie sang into the microphone and before long, they began to sound like a real pop group. "Now we need a cool name for the band," said Milly.

"How about Four Funky Friends?" suggested Sadie. Everyone thought it was a brilliant name, but they still couldn't agree about what to wear on stage.

Milly was sure that bright colors looked best, but Kayla thought frilly clothes were much cooler. "It's got to be something super-stylish," said Charlotte, who always liked to dress in the latest fashion.

Sadie thought for a moment. "We don't have to wear the same thing," she pointed out to the other girls. "Let's all wear our own outfits."

"We could add matching hair accessories," suggested Charlotte.

The friends set to work choosing their clothes and giving each other cool, pop-star hairstyles. Then, they started rehearsing their dance moves. It was trickier than it looked to play an instrument and dance at the same time. The girls kept getting muddled up and tripping over, so they decided to keep the routine really simple.

For the next few weeks, Sadie and her friends spent all their spare time rehearsing. When the big day finally arrived, they couldn't wait to get to the competition. "It's going to be amazing walking out on stage and singing to a real audience," said Sadie, bouncing up and down in the car.

Sadie was so excited, but when they got to the contest and saw the other bands she began to feel worried. They were all much older than the girls and looked very professional with their electric guitars and matching outfits. "I'm a bit nervous," admitted Milly, as she peeked round the curtain at the audience and the judges. "Me too," agreed the other girls.

Sadie knew this might be her one shot at stardom, but she didn't want her friends to feel unhappy. "Let's just go on stage and have fun," she said. "It doesn't matter if we win the competition or not. We've had such a great time starting a band and playing together."

Feeling less nervous, the four friends walked out on stage and started to perform. They had rehearsed so well that every note was perfect and even the dance routine went smoothly. When they finished, the audience clapped and cheered loudly and the girls were so happy that they couldn't stop smiling.

At the end of the contest, the four friends waited anxiously for the winner to be announced. Sadie kept her fingers crossed, but she knew that the other bands had been playing together much longer. Some of the performers were so good Sadie had even asked for their autographs. So, she wasn't really surprised when first prize was given to another group.

"Never mind," said Sadie, as she and her friends clapped and cheered for the winning group. "We've had a brilliant time." They started packing away their instruments, but the judge hadn't finished announcing the winners.

"There is one more award tonight," said the judge. "It's the prize for the most original performance and the winner is… Four Funky Friends."
The girls were so shocked, they stood still and stared at each other. It was only when the audience started cheering again that they realised they needed to go and collect their trophy. "I hope you'll come back next year and play for us again," the judge said, as she shook their hands and handed over the trophy.
"Of course," beamed Sadie, waving the trophy triumphantly in the air.
 Her friends looked at each other and smiled. It was going to be a lot of fun rehearsing for next year's competition.

The Wishing Ring

It was the first day of the summer break and Katie was thrilled to be staying at Grandma's house. Her grandma loved to play games and make up stories, so Katie never felt bored when she visited.

Sometimes, she even thought there was something a little bit magical about Grandma. With her twinkly eyes and merry smile, she looked just like a fairy godmother from a storybook. "Why don't we play dressing-up with the old clothes in the attic?" suggested Grandma when Katie arrived. So, they climbed up the narrow, twisting staircase and opened the door.

"I've always wanted to come up here," said Katie, looking round at the old paintings and boxes. Tiny pieces of dust danced like fairies in the shafts of sunlight. Katie watched them flittering and floating. "Do you believe in fairies?" she asked. "Well," said Grandma, looking thoughtful, "I think that if there is enough magic in the air then you might be lucky and see a fairy." Grandma opened a big trunk and started pulling out wonderful old clothes, long gloves and fancy hats. "Now, let's dress up!" she said with a smile. Katie put on a beautiful dress, a sun hat and a feather boa, while Grandma chose a velvet ball gown.

"How do I look?" asked Katie, striking a pose.

"Very stylish," said Grandma. Katie spun round so that her dress swirled out, but as she turned, she caught sight of something glistening at the bottom of the dressing-up box. She stopped and reached down into the trunk.

"It's an old ring," said Katie, pulling it out and slipping it on her finger. The gold band was a bit too big, but the pink jewel sparkled and shone as she moved her hand.

"That's not just any old ring," said Grandma smiling. "It's a magical wishing ring."

"Let me show you how it works," said Grandma. She placed the ring on her own finger, twisted it round three times and tapped the pink jewel. "I wish I had long, Purple hair."

"Purple hair!" cried Katie, looking confused. The jewel glowed brightly and suddenly, hair began to sprout from Grandma's head. Katie watched as it grew and grew until it nearly touched the floor. "You look so strange, Grandma," she gasped. "That's amazing!"

"Luckily, the magic only lasts until sunset," said Grandma laughing. "Then it wears off and everything goes back to how it was before. I wouldn't want to stay like this. I might get some funny looks at knitting club!"

"It's your turn now," said Grandma, with a twinkle in her eyes. Taking off the ring, she gave it to Katie to put on. "What should I wish for?" wondered Katie. She thought for a moment, then twisted the ring and tapped the jewel just like Grandma had done. In a loud, clear voice she said, "I wish my toys would come to life."

"Ooh, that's a good one," nodded Grandma. "Let's go and see if it's worked." They scampered down the stairs. Katie felt a thrill of excitement as she stood outside her bedroom. Grabbing hold of the handle, she flung open the door.

The room was buzzing with life. Everywhere they looked, Katie and Grandma
could see toys chatting, laughing and walking around. There were dolls dancing
across the carpet and teddies bouncing around.
"Look up there," said Katie, pointing at the bedpost where her cuddly monkey was
swinging by his tail. A flock of fairy dolls fluttered past, giggling and waving their
wands and Katie's rocking horse jumped down from his rockers. He trotted over
to them, neighing happily. "How wonderful," said Grandma, stroking the horse's
furry nose. "Let's join in the fun!" So Katie and Grandma spent an amazing
afternoon playing with the enchanted toys.

Katie was having so much fun, she didn't realise how late it was getting. As the sun began to set, the dolls and teddy bears started turning back into ordinary toys. One by one, they grew silent and still. With the last golden rays of sunlight, the rocking horse climbed back onto his rockers.

Katie looked around at her toys and felt sad. "This has been the best day ever," she said as Grandma tucked her into bed. "If only the magic didn't have to end at sunset."
"Tomorrow is a fresh new day and you can use the wishing ring again," said Grandma. "Now it is time to go to sleep. Sweet dreams." Katie closed her eyes and moments later she was dreaming of all the wonderful things she could wish for the next day.